ALPHA AND OMEGA

Marcel and Paddy Save the Day

Adapted by Tori Kosara

ISBN 978-0-545-21462-9
© 2010 Alpha & Omega Productions, LLC. All Rights Reserved.
Published by Scholastic Inc.
SCHOLASTIC and associated logos are trademarks and/or registered trademarks of Scholastic Inc.

12 11 10 9 8 7 6 5 4 3 2 1   10 11 12 13 14 15/0

Printed in the U.S.A.   40
First printing, September 2010

Scholastic Inc.

New York   Toronto   London   Auckland
Sydney   Mexico City   New Delhi   Hong Kong

Dear Readers,

I'm Justin Long, one of the stars of *Alpha and Omega*. I play Humphrey in the movie, and I hope you enjoyed it. It was a really fun movie to watch and to film. But I loved working on *Alpha and Omega* because it is all about animals and the environment!

Wolves and other animals in many parts of the world are having lots of trouble finding food and safe places to live. But you can help! Ask your teacher or librarian to help you search for local organizations that protect wildlife in your area. They always need volunteers and you can make a difference, no matter how old you are! Animals like Marcel and Humphrey will be thanking you!

I hope you enjoy this great story based on the movie!

Your friend,

Justin Long

Justin

CHAPTER 1

Marcel the goose and his friend, a duck named Paddy, were playing golf in Sawtooth National Wilderness on a bright spring day.

Thwack! Marcel hit the ball and missed the hole. He wanted the shot to count.

"Well, technically it might have gone in, but it didn't," argued Paddy.

The two golfers were debating Marcel's score when two giant shadows appeared. Paddy noticed first and flapped about. Marcel's eyes opened wide. Before them stood two large wolves!

Paddy and Marcel were scared, and tried to
fly away. They weren't used to seeing wolves in
Sawtooth! But the wolves were very quick, and
they caught Marcel and Paddy. Luckily these were
friendly wolves. They just wanted some help.

"We just want to ask you a few questions," said the boy wolf named Humphrey.

The other wolf, Kate, asked, "Where are we?"

Marcel and Paddy told Kate and Humphrey that they were in Sawtooth National Wilderness, a park in Idaho. The wolves could not believe their ears! They were from Jasper Park in Canada. The wolves were a long way from home. Humans had taken them from their home and brought them to Sawtooth because there weren't many wolves left in Idaho.

"We have to get home!" Kate exclaimed. Kate was worried because she had a very important duty back in Canada. She was supposed to unite the two wolf packs at Jasper Park by marrying Garth, a wolf from the other pack.

Marcel and Paddy liked Jasper Park, and wanted to help their new friends. They knew just how to help the wolves get home! "Of course I will help!" said Marcel.

The group set off for Jasper Park.

CHAPTER 2

"Quick! Get in!" Paddy whispered to Humphrey and Kate. They were sneaking into the back of a camper. Marcel and Paddy knew that the humans who owned the camper were headed for Jasper Park.

"Good luck, you two!" yelled Marcel as the camper drove away.

Of course, Paddy and Marcel weren't going to let Kate and Humphrey go on an adventure without them! They would be flying along overhead.

CHAPTER 3

The camper stopped at a rest area.
"Finally!" Humprey said. He
bounded out of the camper for a break.
On his way back, Humphrey found
some cupcakes in the trash. But a
human spotted him and ran to get his
gun. Humphrey was really in trouble.

Just then, Paddy and Marcel appeared!
Marcel used his best golf swing to hit a rock
at the humans, but he missed.

That got Kate's attention. She leapt out of the camper to save Humphrey. The friends were safe, but the camper pulled away without them. Kate and Humphrey slipped sadly into the woods to start walking.

CHAPTER 4

Humphrey and Kate stopped in the woods to rest for the night. That night, Humphrey realized that he was falling in love with Kate.

In the morning, Marcel and Paddy surprised them again. They had found another way for the wolves to get home.

"The Canadian Express shoots right by Jasper Park," Paddy told them. "It's just on the other side of that mountain."

So, the wolves headed off to catch their train home.

CHAPTER 5

Paddy and
Marcel flew along
to keep an eye on
their friends. They were very
worried. Finally, they saw the wolves
jump safely onto a train car.

Later, when Humphrey looked out of the train
to see where they were, he saw his new friends,
Marcel and Paddy, flying alongside them.

CHAPTER 6

The wolves finally made it back home, thanks to their feathered friends. Kate headed straight back to her family. She knew that she must

still unite the two packs, even
though she really wanted to marry
Humphrey instead!

Paddy and Marcel had followed Kate and Humphrey to Jasper. When they saw that everyone was safe, they decided to enjoy a game of golf.

Just as the two birds were about to begin,
Humphrey told them that he was going to run
away from Jasper. Humphrey could not watch
Kate marry another wolf. Broken-hearted, he
headed for the train. Paddy and Marcel were sad,
too. They had hoped their wolf friends would end
up together!

CHAPTER 7

But as Humphrey was leaving, there was a stampede!

Kate and Humphrey quickly worked together to save the packs.

Luckily, Kate and Garth's parents, Tony and Winston, told them that they didn't have to get married. Instead, Kate's sister, Lilly, married Garth

because they were in love. Kate and Humphrey could get married, and the packs would still be united!

Marcel and Paddy were thrilled that their two good friends would be together forever.

Everyone was happy. With the packs united, Winston and Tony could retire and leave Garth and Kate in charge. Paddy and Marcel swooped in once again, this time to teach Tony and Winston to play golf. Happy to be with all of their friends at Jasper, Marcel and Paddy felt like they'd hit a hole in one!